LITTLE MISS BOSSY
BOSSY
and the magic word

Original concept by Roger Hargreaves
Illustrated and written by Adam Hargreaves

MR. MEN   LITTLE MISS

Little Miss Bossy is bossy.

Bossier than the bossiest person you know.

She is also very rude.

Nearly as rude as Mr Uppity, which is very rude indeed.

She never says please.

And she never says thank you.

3 Great Offers for MR.MEN Fans!

MR.MEN TOKEN

1 New Mr. Men or Little Miss Library Bus Presentation Cases

A brand new stronger, roomier school bus library box, with sturdy carrying handle and stay-closed fasteners.
The full colour, wipe-clean boxes make a great home for your full collection.
They're just £5.99 inc P&P and free bookmark!

☐ MR. MEN   ☐ LITTLE MISS (please tick and order overleaf)

2 Door Hangers and Posters

In every Mr. Men and Little Miss book like this one, you will find a special token. Collect 6 tokens and we will send you a brilliant Mr. Men or Little Miss poster and a Mr. Men or Little Miss double sided full colour bedroom door hanger of your choice. Simply tick your choice in the list and tape a 50p coin for your two items to this page.

PLEASE STICK YOUR 50P COIN HERE

Door Hangers (please tick)
☐ Mr. Nosey & Mr. Muddle
☐ Mr. Slow & Mr. Busy
☐ Mr. Messy & Mr. Quiet
☐ Mr. Perfect & Mr. Forgetful
☐ Little Miss Fun & Little Miss Late
☐ Little Miss Helpful & Little Miss Tidy
☐ Little Miss Busy & Little Miss Brainy
☐ Little Miss Star & Little Miss Fun

Posters (please tick)
☐ MR.MEN
☐ LITTLE MISS

CUT ALONG DOTTED LINE AND RETURN THIS WHOLE PAGE

3 Sixteen Beautiful Fridge Magnets – any 2 for £2.00! inc.P&P

They're very special collector's items!
Simply tick your first and second* choices from the list below
of any 2 characters!

1st Choice

- ☐ Mr. Happy
- ☐ Mr. Lazy
- ☐ Mr. Topsy-Turvy
- ☐ Mr. Bounce
- ☐ Mr. Bump
- ☐ Mr. Small
- ☐ Mr. Snow
- ☐ Mr. Wrong

- ☐ Mr. Daydream
- ☐ Mr. Tickle
- ☐ Mr. Greedy
- ☐ Mr. Funny
- ☐ Little Miss Giggles
- ☐ Little Miss Splendid
- ☐ Little Miss Naughty
- ☐ Little Miss Sunshine

2nd Choice

- ☐ Mr. Happy
- ☐ Mr. Lazy
- ☐ Mr. Topsy-Turvy
- ☐ Mr. Bounce
- ☐ Mr. Bump
- ☐ Mr. Small
- ☐ Mr. Snow
- ☐ Mr. Wrong

- ☐ Mr. Daydream
- ☐ Mr. Tickle
- ☐ Mr. Greedy
- ☐ Mr. Funny
- ☐ Little Miss Giggles
- ☐ Little Miss Splendid
- ☐ Little Miss Naughty
- ☐ Little Miss Sunshine

*Only in case your first choice is out of stock.

— TO BE COMPLETED BY AN ADULT —

**To apply for any of these great offers, ask an adult to complete the coupon below and send it with
the appropriate payment and tokens, if needed, to MR. MEN OFFERS, PO BOX 7, MANCHESTER M19 2HD**

☐ Please send ____ Mr. Men Library case(s) and/or ____ Little Miss Library case(s) at £5.99 each inc P&P

☐ Please send a poster and door hanger as selected overleaf. I enclose six tokens plus a 50p coin for P&P

☐ Please send me ____ pair(s) of Mr. Men/Little Miss fridge magnets, as selected above at £2.00 inc P&P

Fan's Name _____

Address _____

_____ **Postcode** _____

Date of Birth _____

Name of Parent/Guardian _____

Total amount enclosed £_____

☐ **I enclose a cheque/postal order payable to Egmont Books Limited**

☐ **Please charge my MasterCard/Visa/Amex/Switch or Delta account** (delete as appropriate)

Card Number

Expiry date ____/____   **Signature** _____

Please allow 28 days for delivery. We reserve the right to change the terms of this offer at any time
but we offer a 14 day money back guarantee. This does not affect your statutory rights.

MR.MEN   LITTLE MISS
Mr. Men and Little Miss™ & ©Mrs. Roger Hargreaves

CUT ALONG DOTTED LINE AND RETURN THIS WHOLE PAGE

Like the time she met Mr Sneeze.

"ATISHOO!" sneezed Mr Sneeze.

"Stop sneezing!" ordered Miss Bossy.

"I can't, ATISHOO!, help it," replied Mr Sneeze.

"Nonsense!" said Miss Bossy.

Like the time she met Little Miss Chatterbox.

"Good morning," said Miss Chatterbox. " Lovely day isn't it? Just the right weather for a walk. Talking about the weather...."

"Be quiet!" ordered Miss Bossy.

And like the time she tripped over Mr Small.

"You're too small!" exclaimed Miss Bossy, "Grow up!"

"I can't," said Mr Small.

"Then get out of my way in future!" ordered Miss Bossy.

2

Poor Mr Sneeze.

Poor Little Miss Chatterbox.

And poor Mr Small.

It was Mr Small who decided that something had to be done.

He went to see Little Miss Magic.

And once he had explained the problem she agreed to teach Miss Bossy a lesson.

"... and I think I know just how to do it," she replied.

The next day Little Miss Bossy bumped into Mr Greedy.

"You're too big," she cried. "Lose some weight!"

At the same time Little Miss Magic, who had followed Miss Bossy, muttered a very magic word.

And do you know what happened?

Of course you don't...

... but you do now!

"Who are you calling big," laughed Mr Greedy. "You ought to take a look at yourself!"

Little Miss Bossy was lost for words.

As soon as Mr Greedy had gone Miss Magic muttered some more magic words and Miss Bossy returned to normal.

Further down the lane Miss Bossy passed Mr Cheerful's gate. He was painting stripes on his house to cheer it up.

"That looks ridiculous," snapped Miss Bossy. "Paint over those stripes!"

Little Miss Magic whispered the very magic word again.

Mr Cheerful started to chuckle.

"You ought to look at yourself," he laughed.

Miss Bossy did.

She was covered in stripes!

From her hiding place Little Miss Magic smiled to herself.

Next, she met Little Miss Splendid.

"What a stupid hat," she said. "Go and put on something more sensible!"

Miss Magic uttered the magic word again and I'm sure you can guess what happened next.

"Speak for yourself!" said Miss Splendid, bursting into laughter.

And for the third time that day Little Miss Bossy was lost for words.

Just then Mr Small came along.

"Having a nice day?" he asked.

"Mind your own business, pip-squeak!" snapped Miss Bossy.

"And who are you to call me pip-squeak!" said Mr Small and chuckled.

"Haven't you learnt your lesson yet?"

Miss Magic came out from behind the tree where she had been hiding.

"Oh it's you," squeaked Miss Bossy. "Turn me back to my proper size!"

"You have to say the magic word," replied Miss Magic.

"Abracadabra," squeaked Miss Bossy.

"No, that's not the magic word I was thinking of."

I'm sure you know what the magic word is, but it took Miss Bossy a bit longer to think of it.

"Please," she said eventually.

And did she learn her lesson?

Well, she learnt one lesson.

Little Miss Bossy is still just as bossy as ever, but at least she now says please!

"GO TO SLEEP!"

"please."